LITTLE WOLF

by Ann McGovern

pictures by Nola Langner

SCHOLASTIC BOOK SERVICES
NEW YORK · TORONTO · LONDON · AUCKLAND · SYDNEY

For
    Peter
    Frisky
    Tom
    Lisa
    Josh
    Eli
    Gretchen
    Belinda
    Jack
    Teeta

Copyright © 1965 by Ann McGovern. This edition is published by Scholastic Book Services, a division of Scholastic Magazines, Inc., by arrangement with Abelard-Schuman Limited.

1st printing .... November 1970

Printed in the U.S.A.

It is morning.
The sun begins to rise.

The sun rises higher
and higher in the sky.
It shines on all the houses
of the Indian tribe.

The sun wakes up the mother — Flower Wolf.
And the father — Hunt Wolf.
And the old grandfather — Wise Wolf.
And the boy — Little Wolf.

Another day has come.
Flower Wolf will cook.
Hunt Wolf will hunt.
Wise Wolf will sit by the fire.

And Little Wolf,
Little Wolf will go to the woods.

But Little Wolf will not please his father.
For he will not hunt
like all the other boys in the tribe.
Little Wolf is not a hunter.

He brings home animals that cannot run
and birds that cannot fly.
He cares for them and makes them well again.

Now Hunt Wolf roars
like the angry thunder god.
"Today, you will hunt!"
he commands Little Wolf.
Little Wolf looks up at his father.

"You are brave," his father says.
"I have seen you wrestle with Big Knife.
But what good is your bravery if you do not
face the sharp antlers of the deer?

"You are swift.
I have seen you race Fast-as-the-Wind.
But what good is your swiftness
if you do not follow the fleeing rabbit?

"You are wise.
You know when rain will fall
and where the big fish swim.
But what good is your wisdom
if you do not trick the sly fox?

"You are brave. And swift. And wise.
You are all these things.
But all these things are nothing
if you do not hunt!"

Now Wise Wolf speaks.
"I know we must kill animals," he says.
"Our people would die if we did not hunt for food.
But let the boy be.
There are other ways."

Hunt Wolf shakes his head.
"No! My son shames me."

"Go now!" he tells Little Wolf.
"And come home when you have killed a deer
or a rabbit or a fox."

So Little Wolf takes his bow and arrow
and leaves his house.
He walks by the houses of all the hunters.
He walks by the Chief's house.
He sees the Chief's only son, Brave Bear.
Brave Bear is very small,
but he is going to be a mighty hunter.

Little Wolf greets the Chief and his son.
But they do not speak to him,
for Little Wolf is not a hunter
like all the other boys in the tribe.

Little Wolf goes to the woods.
Everything is very green.
Everything is very quiet.

He knows the woods well.
Wise Wolf has taught him
the ways of the woods.
He has taught him about the animals
and about the plants that grow
in the green, quiet woods.

Plants that make men sick,
and plants that make men well.

Soon Little Wolf sees two big brown eyes.
The big brown eyes of a deer.

Little Wolf throws down his bow and arrow.
"How can I be a hunter?" he asks softly.
"How can I be a hunter, if I have to kill you?"

The deer is dark brown velvet running deep
into the woods.

Then Little Wolf sees a round white tail.
The round white tail of a rabbit.

"I will not be a hunter," he says softly.
"I will not be a hunter if I have to kill you."

The rabbit is a quick quiver in the grass,
and is gone.

Then Little Wolf sees a long nose.
The long nose of a fox.

"Never, never will I hunt," he says.
"Never, never will I hunt if I have to kill you."

Then Little Wolf sees the tail of the fox.
It is caught in a trap.

Little Wolf opens the trap and sets the fox free.

The fox is a bounding blur of bright copper.

Now it is night.
The moon begins to rise.
The moon rises higher and higher in the sky.
It shines on all the houses
of the Indian tribe.

The moon shines on the mother — Flower Wolf.
And on the father — Hunt Wolf.
And on the old grandfather — Wise Wolf.

And on the boy — Little Wolf.

Little Wolf is leaving the woods.
The dark quiet woods.
The trees standing close to the moon.
The plants sleeping near to the earth.

Little Wolf has nothing to show his father.
No deer. No rabbit. No fox.
But he is going home.

Then, in the dark quiet night,
he hears a cry.
Little Wolf moves quickly, quietly.
He follows the sound of the cry.

There, under the giant oak,
lies Brave Bear, the Chief's only son.

Brave Bear cries out, "I am dying.
The pain is like a hundred arrows
shooting through me."

Little Wolf sees some berries lying near.
He knows these are berries that make men sick.
He knows Brave Bear has eaten the berries.

"Run for help," Brave Bear moans.
"Run for my father—hurry!"

"I can help you," Little Wolf says.
"You?" Brave Bear says.
"What can *you* do? My father says
you cannot even hunt!"

Little Wolf says, "I know the secrets
of the woods.
I can help you."

Little Wolf leaves Brave Bear.
Soon, he returns
with grasses and herbs.

"Eat these," Little Wolf says,
"and you will be well
when the sun shines again."

All night, Little Wolf stays with Brave Bear.
The two boys sleep in the woods.
In the moon-filled quiet woods.

Now it is the morning
of the next day.
The sun begins to rise.
The sun rises higher
and higher in the sky.

The sun shines on the two boys who are going home.

Brave Bear goes home with Little Wolf.
He tells Hunt Wolf and Flower Wolf and
Wise Wolf what has happened in the woods.

Hunt Wolf says,
"I am glad you are well, Brave Bear.
Our tribe needs you.
You will be a mighty hunter some day."

Then Hunt Wolf looks at his son and smiles.
"Our tribe needs you, too, Little Wolf.
You will be a mighty healer some day."
And Wise Wolf nods his head.

This day
Flower Wolf will cook.
Hunt Wolf will hunt.

Wise Wolf will sit by the fire.
And Little Wolf,
Little Wolf will go to the woods.

He will not kill the deer
or the rabbit or the fox.
He will see the animals
that run through the woods.
He will watch them.
And he will learn.

He will see the plants
that grow in the woods.
He will study them.
And he will learn.

And that is Little Wolf's way.